VONCOSEL Y. HOYOS

Eternal Obsession

A Novella By

JD MOORES

This Fictionalized Account of a True Story is an Extended Adaptation of the Author's Award Winning Short Screenplay Based on Publicly Documented and Eyewitness Information– Copyright 2016, All Rights Reserved.

First published in the USA by

Woodlane Books /Woodlane Enterprises, LLC © 2016

First Printed & Distributed By CreateSpace.com

Set in Book Antiqua

NOTE: *Though fictionalized and embellished, most of the story, its characters and general content is inspired by actual people and events which are part of the public record (newspapers, court testimony, etc.), upon which most of the non-fiction/non-dramatized portions have been based. All real life subjects-slash-"characters" and their immediate families are now deceased.*

JD MOORES

INTRODUCTION

In 1931, James Whale's iconic film adaptation of Mary Shelley's mad scientist novel *Frankenstein* was considered so potentially disturbing that its producers felt the need to start by having one of the actors walk out onto a literal stage onscreen and warn anyone in the audience that might be squeamish and feint of heart.

At around the same time, a beautiful young woman's life was coming to a slow end even as her caretaker's dream-fueled romantic obsession with her was not only going strong, but about to get kicked into high gear. In the end, his desire and eventual attempt to be with her forever would turn HIM into a real life "mad scientist!"

And yet, when he was finally caught and his story hit the nation's newspapers, the same Depression Era public that squirmed at the sight of Lugosi and Karloff in their iconic movie monster roles seemed to embrace this crazy old man as a brave, almost heroic romantic!

As of this novella's first publication, it has been 75 years since Key West attempted to prosecute him for his acts of... desecration. Besides still being the occasional topic of documentary-style television shows, several writers have blended fact and fiction in books about Count Carl VonCosel and the tragic beauty Elena Hoyos - the most notable among them being authors Ben Harrison, Tom Swicegood, and, well... VonCosel, himself, whose bizarre autobiography graced the pages of the pulp magazine Fantastic Adventures in 1947.

When I first saw the story on a rerun of *Haunted History* back in 2010, I was nowhere near willing to write about it and remained that way for almost two years. Then, in 2012, I suddenly came up with an angle and an irresistible impulse to explore it. That angle has as much to do with the public's reaction to VonCosel and what he did as with the story, itself. In fact, compared with VonCosel's, I eventually came to regard the actions and reactions of the Key West people and authorities as being equally if not more bizarre, duplicitous, and disrespectful.

To my mild surprise, the script and its angle seems to work, earning the praise of a Hollywood screenwriter in my current hometown and a prize in national competition. Here's hoping it works as well in prose.

- JD Moores, Author...2015

ALERT: What follows are the last recorded words of a missing person. Though they offer another person's story and perspective, they also serve as a limited, yet potentially personal and thus valuable glimpse into the subject's psyche just before their disappearance... 75 years ago.

*   *   *

PROLOGUE

It began when my editor spoke of a dramatically different story he wished me to cover. I write about world affairs, so I wearily asked for more details, expecting another depressing development from war torn Europe and cringing at the thought of having to write about it again for an isolationist readership. Instead, my editor said, "It's about lovers from Germany and Cuba in Key West."

I needed hear no more. Before I knew it, I was aboard a train, zooming down Florida's East Coast Railway and devouring all of the information I had been provided on the matter. There wasn't much, but what there was had an effect. Key West is a hot place that rarely experiences a shift in climate more than about fifteen to twenty degrees, yet upon stepping off the train in eighty degree weather, the first thing I did was shiver.

There was definitely an energy about town – that almost indescribable sense that something has happened. The locals were talking in whispers loud and soft and I know I spotted more than two or three like myself.

Instead of taking a cab, I chose to walk the busy streets, making my rounds to all of the places I had to go before approaching the source. Among them was the courthouse, the Marine Hospital, and the Lopez Funeral Home, which I learned from the owner had just recently been packed with over a thousand people, including schoolchildren. I naively asked if there had been a big funeral. The owner smirked, then asked if I had really not been told already. I said no, but then excused myself before he could explain, thanking him for his time and cooperation.

It is one thing to know the cold, hard facts, but faced with the essence of the story, I felt like I was about to be led down a rabbit hole of mostly morbid gossip. So, I decided to skip the formalities and go straight to the source, which meant talking to the only one of those two lovers still available to me. That meant going to only one place.

Jail.

I was led inside by a guard who warned me with an annoyingly thick accent about the degenerate prisoner I was about to meet. "Here he is," he said as we turned a corner. "The Sheriff seems to like the guy, but, uh... Well, just don't say I didn't warn 'ya."

When the guard finally left, I found and pulled an old chair up to the bars, and sat down. I initially had a hard time seeing the prisoner clearly as he seemed to stay as far back and away from the bars as possible. When I did, though, I was a bit taken aback. This gaunt, silver-haired, bearded old man was peering at me through spectacles. - or over them. It was hard to tell. He seemed incredibly out of place and with a distinct German accent, spoke with a fairly weak voice.

"Who are you with?" he asked.

Immediately, I knew he had been visited by other reporters and probably did not look forward to more. "I'm... alone," I said, which was technically the truth.

"Forgive me, but I have nothing to say."

I could see him retreating as far as he could into his already cramped cell as I struggled to think of a useful response. Then, I gave in to my own frustration and gambled.

"Then you must forgive me," I said, "because I don't believe you." His head rose. It got his attention. "I'm sorry," I said, "but I won't buy into the lonely recluse routine. Besides, I think you want to explain yourself. I think you're desperate to explain, and to someone other than a police officer or an analyst."

"Or a reporter," he replied, his voice strengthened with frustration. I had no comeback, but it was just as well. Whether or not he admitted it, I had hit a nerve. Sure enough, his voice returned to normal as he asked the one question I knew I had to answer before he would trust me. "Do you think I'm crazy?"

"Apparently, nobody else does," I said. "Why should I?"

He paused for a moment, then asked, "Have you ever lost someone? Have you ever had someone... taken from you?"

It was a calculated and intentionally dramatic question, but I felt I had to be completely honest. "Yes," I said, "In '37. It was an accident."

"My loss was not an accident," he said bitterly, "And it has not been nine years since it happened despite what some insist is the truth. Of course, I don't expect you or anyone to understand - not with your narrow definitions of life and... and death."

"I have no hard and fast definitions of my own for those things," I said, hardly aware that I had started speaking before hearing myself. "It's like... if something doesn't move or talk, is it not there? If something can't be seen or... or heard, does it not exist? You would think an entire nation of people who believe there's a god would have an easier time understanding us."

Then, I stopped. What had I said? That was what immediately crossed my mind. I was about to apologize for my lack of professionalism and possible incoherence when I noticed him moving closer to the bars and nodding.

"If I tell you," he began in a halting tone. "If I tell you everything, honestly... what will you say?"

I tried to put thought into my response, but could only conjure two words. "The truth."

Within moments, he began his tale. In all, it took less time than I anticipated, but then the authorities were not going to let me stay all of that or any other day. I had no recording device and took no dictation, so the best I can do is narrate from my incredibly strong memory and from the other newspaper coverage up to now.

Public opinion here in the Keys appears to be split, with a mixture of sympathy and revulsion brewing and not much in between. A hearing is to be held on the case in November and the prisoner has been deemed sane and able to stand trial. I hope it's a fair one that places everyone's testimony in the proper context because I think there's an element here – maybe even a fundamental truth - that is being overlooked, perhaps intentionally. I'm not a novelist, but in order to convey what I mean as I tell the story, I have to dramatize.

By the time he finished his tale, I felt like a different person. As I said, I shivered upon arrival, mostly because all I knew were the plain facts, but fact in this story is almost beside the point. You cannot understand what has happened here and why if you only look at and pay attention to the facts. Call that double-talk or nonsense if you will. I'm sure my editor would were I dumb enough to speak this way in front of him.

You, however... you're in a different position, one unique compared with most that will read my coverage. I only hope that means you understand, as I do, the series of events, the man at its center and awaiting trial, and the obsession that began so long ago that I feel it may well be... eternal.

CHAPTER ONE

With his fingers around the stethoscope and the stethoscope pressed to her chest, Carl VonCosel could almost feel the beating of Elena's heart reverberate through his own body. To him, every beat validated a lifetime of predictions and signs pointing to their inevitable meeting. At 53 years of age, it had been a while since he had felt anything quite like it.

She's here. She's really here — the young woman that had appeared to me like a ghost, at home, on the boat and in places around the world — sitting before me. It was intoxicating.

Then, after the last deep breath, the coughing began. She was clearly trying to cough as quietly, discreetly, and ladylike as possible. As she stopped and removed it from her mouth, however, it was VonCosel's turn to feel his own heart skip a beat at the sight of those few, yet visible flecks of red on Elena's handkerchief.

It was blood - another sign of what he knew the tests would show. In that moment, Elena looked up at him, her big, brown eyes seeming to beg for answers... or, at least, hope. He could give one of those things, but not the other, and unfortunately, it would be of no comfort whatsoever.

"Doctor VonCosel?" The voice of a nurse now standing in the doorway startled and even frustrated him. It was a fact he had no intention of hiding as he looked in the nurse's direction. "Doctor Tanzler wanted me to give you these," she said. "They're the last of Ms. Hoyos' test results."

With a grimace, VonCosel took the chart from the nurse's hand and looked at the results. They confirmed what he already knew. They also included the irritating fact which the nurse had left out – that Elena Hoyos' real name was Elena Hoyos Mesa.

"Was this what you expected?" the nurse asked.

VonCosel wanted to throw the clipboard back in the nurse's face in anger. Nevertheless... "Thank you," he said as he casually handed back the test results. Fortunately, the nurse promptly left the room.

"Mama waits for us," Elena said as VonCosel turned back around to face her.

It was all VonCosel could do not to run his fingers through her ebony hair and his hand down her neck and across her shoulder. At the last second, he noticed that one of his hands had started moving from its place at his side. He quickly withdrew, but not before Elena seemed to notice. Again, she made eye contact, but this time, it seemed more intentional and a bit less... innocent. Be it wishful thinking or insightful perception, VonCosel could only think one thing: She knew.

Elena knew.

Like the exam room, the corridor of the Marine Hospital seemed cold and even a bit oppressive with its walls of concrete blocks and stark, off-white coloring. For a moment, it made VonCosel forget the myriad of conflicting and inconvenient inclinations he felt towards his patient. He felt sorry for the older woman standing before him. It was Elena's mother Aurora, and her facial expression was one of a person waiting to hear bad news.

"The results are back," he said. "We've confirmed tuberculosis. I'm sorry."

Aurora took a quick, deep breath and let out a sigh of resignation. TB had been like a plague in certain parts of the country, its ravaging effects well-documented. Surely, she knew what was to come. "My poor girl," she said, as if musing to herself. "First, the baby, then Luis... both gone. Our family business is suffering and now this..." This already grieving mother – who, ironically, was younger than VonCosel - dabbed at the corner of one moist eye.

VonCosel's mixed feelings were palpable. He could not help but see this as his chance to employ a calculated gamble aimed not just at prolonging Elena's life, but also his time with her, at her side. "There isn't much that anyone can do here," VonCosel began in a halting tone, "but... if you're willing, I can offer some alternative and... experimental treatments – perhaps even in your own home. There have long been indications that electricity, for example, might stimulate the body and arrest the advancement of certain... conditions."

As Aurora took a moment to think, Elena appeared in the exam room's open doorway. As VonCosel and Aurora looked over at her, Elena nodded softly as if to confirm that she had heard what he said and agreed to the terms. With that, VonCosel looked back at Aurora, who also nodded in agreement.

It was settled, yet once again, VonCosel had to reconcile two mindsets. Though he believed he was on the right track, medically speaking, he admits that it was probably closer to the truth to say that he wasn't so much buying time as he was stealing... or sharing... what little time Elena had left.

*   *   *

Carl VonCosel described the circumstances.

> *In the Marine Hospital where I worked, there was a ward which held most of our patients with TB, still frequently called consumption. I saw far too many patients afflicted by the disease. Before the day we met, I had merely considered such places an unfortunate necessity, both for the patients that needed round-the-clock care and for any friends and family which might contract the disease in close proximity. Afterwards, I trembled in sadness at the thought of this angelic girl being forced to live out her days among the other poor souls afflicted by this wretched condition. If anyone was motivated to find a cure, I was; but for the time being, keeping Elena out of that crowded and noisy hell of loud moans and bone-rattling coughs... That was my first priority.*

He was never chiefly a physician if he was ever a physician at all. Claiming to have no fewer than nine college degrees, his skills seem mostly relegated to engineering and working with electricity. On a small plot of land sat an unfinished airplane which he claims to have constructed, himself, and which he rechristened in Elena's honor. Having already traveled the world and even resided in a concentration camp for war refugees in Australia, this plane was intended to take he and Elena on their own trip around the world with particular emphasis upon touring the South Pacific.

So when it came to his attempts to cure Elena, his treatments and prescriptions were largely homeopathic in between experiments with radiation and electrical stimulation. Like the airplane, he even constructed the equipment, himself – if not in the Hoyos' home, then in a shack nearby where he temporarily resided. He claimed that it was working and would have worked better had the environment and the family's attitude been different, but Elena's close knit family allegedly watched her accept elaborate gifts from VonCosel, then abruptly deny her illness and forbade them to meet. The gifts would disappear. In essence, she could be ill, he said, but only on their terms. Only when it was convenient and potentially profitable to the family.

It was disheartening, but not altogether surprising. Those were the earliest days of an ongoing economic depression. It has been hard on everyone, but as a fellow immigrant, himself, he could imagine the added hardships of a large immigrant family whose livelihood in the cigar trade has not only been hurt by the rise of cigarettes, but which may be slowly killing the entire Hoyos family.

After years of visions and signs of this raven-haired beauty, promised in a boyhood dream to be the love of his life by his notable ancestor the Countess VonCosel, Carl VonCosel finally had the real thing in Elena. She existed, they knew each other, and so far, they seemed to get along. However, if this was the fulfillment of a personal prophecy, it came with a number of strings attached.

The first was that Hoyos was no longer her only last name. Legally, she was Maria Elena Millagro Hoyos-Mesa, roughly 22 years old, and still married to a man named Luis with whom she had conceived and recently miscarried. Though he had not accompanied her to the Marine Hospital, she still wore a conspicuous-enough wedding ring, so despite Aurora's assertion that he was lost to them, it was unclear as yet just how much of a presence Luis was going to be.

For VonCosel, the moral and ethical complications were clear, yet easily overlooked. He, too, had belonged to another, as he put it, but in any case, what Elena meant in the overall arc of VonCosel's life seemed far more important. After all, it predated Elena, herself, by more than thirty years. It made their initial meeting seem like divine providence. All of this is something VonCosel is quick to use and latch onto as a means of justifying his position and perspective.

In the eyes of the law, I knew she belonged to another, but did I not also belong to another at one time? We came from different worlds, yet understood each other in ways that had nothing to do with where either of us were from. What could possibly be more important?

Another free radical in this equation was Elena's family and her surprisingly limited social world, which was not all that large as usual Hispanic families go. It was Elena, her parents, and her two sisters – Florinda and Celia - plus the occasional visits by members of their extended family as well as friends and co-workers. Still, the household was almost never lacking for company. Key West has a particularly strong Cuban presence and is actually closer to Cuba than to Florida, the American state of which it is legally part. Add to that the fact that Elena's father is a successful or once-successful businessman in a fairly small community and you have a recipe for a full house almost 'round-the-clock.

As such, even the very gentle and ladylike Elena was anything but a kept little princess. In her adolescence, she had been recognizable around town as that beautiful girl with the flower in her hair who danced her heart out at the Cuban Club. As immigrants go, her family had been fairly successful in business thanks to her father's cigar shop. Now, despite her condition, it was this family which demanded the most from her in just about every respect.

VonCosel saw this firsthand while visiting in the evenings. For a private, middle-aged European man that had lived alone for most of his life, integrating himself in Hoyos family social gatherings had to appear daunting and maybe even embarrassing. In the already small Hoyos home on a hot Key West evening was this presumably educated and silver-haired German man of advancing years trying not to stick out like a sore thumb among a dozen or so Spanish-speaking and somewhat swarthy, cigar-smoking Cubans.

The smoking alone was bad enough. It was a culturally ingrained habit of the men, in particular, which VonCosel knew he was never going to successfully discourage let alone stop. Besides, many in Europe shared the habit or one similar. Almost as alarming given Elena's condition was the way she was still being forced into playing hostess for her boisterous familia. Even in such a small place, it was a rigorous job, and even as a married woman in her early twenties, she was still clearly treated like the child that is best seen, yet rarely heard. As VonCosel put it:

I was included at first, reminded of the time I passed through Cuba, so I knew some of what to expect. That small and embattled little country to the South is still colorful and high-spirited, all of which was reflected in the Hoyos household. Still, it pained me to watch Elena – whom I knew to be so easily fatigued in her condition – be forced to wait on this loud and rambunctious bunch and inhale their noxious cigar smoke.

In fairness, it could not have been easy on Elena, either. Besides the physical work, she was essentially juggling the strong, yet vastly different and even somewhat unclear affections of both her family and, now, VonCosel, whose dual role as her doctor and self-appointed friend and part-time guardian must have been confusing and, at times, unsettling. Yet, like so many women, she is alleged to have often handled both with little more than her well-known smile.

Still, her guard had to come down at some point. On a particularly busy evening in the Hoyos home, VonCosel recalls Elena taking a moment to sit before a window overlooking the street. At one point, as one of many vehicles passed, she mused, "There he goes."

VonCosel asked who she was talking about and, with a sad sigh, Elena replied, "Luis... my husband. But he lives with another now." Quietly, VonCosel watched as Elena hung her head and, in what he knew was one of Elena's rare private moments, she muttered in Spanish, "Adios, mi amor perdido."

Though bittersweet, the moment gave VonCosel the answer he needed, both literally and figuratively. Whatever the law still had to say on their marriage, Luis was gone. In the days ahead, VonCosel would learn more, but a moment after watching Elena quietly bid farewell to her husband, he was once again watching her run herself ragged by waiting on her mother, her father, and what were mostly his friends.

Finally, VonCosel could take it no more. As Elena passed where he sat, he quickly reached out and touched her hand. Ever the courteous hostess, Elena stopped and looked at him with a tired smile. "Elena," he began, "I admire you for trying, but all this running around, this noise and excitement..." Wary of being overheard, VonCosel recalls measuring his words carefully. "No offense, my darling, but... your condition," he continued in what was more of a loud whisper. "I'm concerned. Estoy preoccupada."

His comment bordered on the intrusive and potentially condescending, but it could not be avoided. Fortunately, he knew that whether warranted or not, Elena would never openly take offense.

"I am okay, doctor," she said. "After all, they are my family. What can I do?" Then, it was her turn to show concern as she reached down and touched his hand, reassuring him as she did. "Don't worry. I can rest later."

VonCosel began to protest, but barely managed a single word before being stopped. "Please," Elena interrupted. "Understand," she said, "and suffer this for me. Por favor."

And so he did, VonCosel says, suffering for her the present while being anxious about the future. It was a phrase she would say on several more occasions during their time together, which rapidly came to feel like one of their things as a couple. Yet it was intensely bittersweet at the same time and an ongoing reminder that when he looked into her eyes, he was looking into a radiant flame being slowly, but surely suffocated out of existence.

JD MOORES

CHAPTER TWO

As time progressed, so did Elena's illness, but it did so in fits and starts which continued to convince the family sometimes that she had been cured or was not really sick at all. Despite the confidence VonCosel had in his alternative and electrified treatments, he knew better. Modern medicine has no cure, and he knew that even if he were to stumble upon it, were he too late, he may never know. Neither would Elena.

Courting Elena was always going to be tricky business. Though an adult, she was not even half his age. To his mild chagrin, this would often prompt her to call him Pops or Poppy, especially in mixed company. In her innocence, she would explain herself by remarking that VonCosel looked even older than her own father!

When Elena felt well, they would take walks together and, on at least one occasion, he showed her the plane he was building. He told her of his adventures so far and made romantic promises about how the two of them would see the world together as they soared across the seven seas in the craft which he now referred to as La Condesa de Cosel.

It was an overture of sorts to Elena revealing VonCosel's intent to marry her, which he believes she understood. So when Elena would smile and counter with an alternative name, VonCosel merely overlooked it as being the excited talk of a still young woman that was even younger at heart. To his mind, it could never be her way of subtly cluing him into the obvious – that she was not his child bride, as he referred to her, and for many a reason, would likely never be.

On the days she felt ill, he would sit by her humble wooden bed and they would talk as she just barely managed a snack consisting mostly of some fruit he would bring to her. Again and again, he would bring her gifts of jewelry and clothing, yet again and again, he would have to face down her family as they would make excuses as to why Elena was not wearing them or was only wearing one piece. They would tell him that she had rejected the gifts and that they had been sold or given away. As such, they would also tell him that his services were no longer needed and it would be more appropriate were he to leave and not come back.

However, VonCosel would come back, and as time passed, he found the strength he needed to confront the family that seemed to care less about their daughter and sibling than their social reputation and financial well-being. To a degree, VonCosel is used to being regarded with less than welcoming attitudes. He is, after all, a German in a nation which blames Germany for the Great War and will no doubt blame it even more should we find ourselves embroiled in another global conflict beginning mostly in Europe. What roiled him was the effect that their actions and attitudes had on Elena both physically and emotionally – made all the worse by the inescapable fact that Elena truly did love them, especially her beloved sisters. At one point, it was Elena, herself, that had to remind VonCosel of her love and loyalty to her family, which came with the heartbreaking suggestion made on at least one occasion that their differences were insurmountable and perhaps their association should end.

Sure enough, VonCosel eventually found himself vacating the shack near the Hoyos home and relocating, as well as spending more and more time in his job at the Marine Hospital. The problem for everyone, of course, was more than just VonCosel's unwillingness to give up the perceived affair. He was, by then, constitutionally incapable.

Fortunately for him, a little time would pass before the family members would abruptly change their minds and beckon him to care for their Elena once again. And once again, VonCosel would heed the calls – even when he knew that there was increasingly little he was either allowed or able to do anymore to effectively treat Elena's Tuberculosis.

No longer was the goal to cure Elena. Now, it was merely to keep her alive as long as possible.

*   *   *

It should be no secret or surprise that Elena's care became more and more challenging as time went on. With her coughing also increased her fatigue, difficulty breathing, and various aches and pains to exacerbate a rapidly diminishing appetite that never bode well for this already wafer thin girl. These symptoms would also alternate with instances in which Elena would believe she was healed or that she never really had TB. However frustrating, VonCosel knew to expect it. In our talks, he mentioned the same occurrence with famed author Anton Chekhov in his last days with the disease.

More and more, VonCosel found it difficult to find time alone with his all-too-mortal beloved. Family friends, including some of her father's friends and business associates, would drop by and even congregate around Elena – even while she lay in bed in her bedroom – talking loudly and, of course, enjoying their cigars. Her father Francisco, nicknamed Pancho, would sit alone by her bedside and talk to her, telling her stories while puffing on his cigar which always delighted Elena.

This, VonCosel understood, of course. He was, after all, her father, and their time together would no doubt be short. Only when it came time for some treatment would VonCosel and Elena finally find the privacy they allegedly craved.

Gone was the bulky electrical and radiology equipment. Instead, VonCosel would simply draw blood and return it to the lab at the Marine Hospital for evaluation. Her TB was going to spread no matter what. At the very least, they could keep track of the rate.

Young and naive as she was, Elena was still from a traditional Catholic family. She knew right from wrong in a Biblical sense and began openly reflecting upon her young life, which had mostly been filled with the frivolity of looking pretty, dancing at the Cuban club, and generally driving the boys of Key West absolutely mad when and wherever the opportunity arose. Though not altogether uncommon, it led to her getting married to Luis while still a teenager. And, it led to the pregnancy and miscarriage that in hindsight, she believed, could have portended the Tuberculosis. That, it seems, is what drove Luis away for good.

Even for the fact that she resided on an already small assembly of islands, Elena's world was getting smaller and smaller with every passing day. This would naturally inspire reflection and self-analysis which, of course, led to guilt amplified by her terminal state. Above her bed supposedly hung a picture of Saint Cecelia, whose tomb VonCosel had visited in Rome. He regards her as his guardian angel and, while there, claims to have witnessed one of his earliest visions of the woman he now believes to be Elena Hoyos.

This sort of thing increasingly found its way into the two's little talks, which was fine for both. Yet, up to then, Elena still regarded him as an elder or, as he put it, a teacher.

This, he was, but more and more, he longed for the day when they would at last become the loving and equal partners he knew they were meant to be.

One afternoon, Elena laid on an ottoman in the Hoyos' living area while VonCosel prepared to draw blood. She seemed particularly tired and uncomfortable even in her reclining state, which seemed to make her breathing sound all the more labored. This all seemed to worry VonCosel, but there was a silver lining.

They were alone. Family was nearby, as always, and the little dog that Elena and her sisters loved so much lie dutifully at her side, wagging its tail and splitting its watchful gaze between the two. These little things were to be ignored, however. Their relationship had to evolve, and there was precious little time left for it to do so.

"How long must we continue the treatments?" Elena asked, eyeing a strange vial of liquid nearby which she had not seen before.

"As I said, my darling, that is entirely up to you."

Elena began toying with her necklace, which pleased VonCosel as he had, of course, been the one to give it to her. "Do you like the gifts?" he asked.

"Very much," she replied, choking up a little afterwards. When the coughing let up, she sighed and let her head fall back as she stared at the ceiling. "Do you think this can ever be cured?"

"Others say no, but medicine is science, my darling, and science is in constant flux. I believe we are stymied only by our fear of the unknown and of failure. The other rs run from aggressive treatment because they are afraid."

"Like Luis," Elena remarked, sounding more mature in the moment than she ever had before.

"I, however, am not afraid," VonCosel said, choosing not to dwell on the mention of Elena's absent husband. "But," he began again, haltingly, "...are you?"

Elena bowed her head. "I was at first," she said. Then, she looked VonCosel squarely in the eyes. "I see how much you do, Doctor. 'How much you seem to care."

"But I do care," VonCosel interrupted, though Elena never missed a beat.

With a smile, she continued, "And how you look at me sometimes."

Again, Elena placed her hand on VonCosel's, but though she pulled it back, she did so more slowly that time. That time, something was different. "I wonder how you must see me," Elena mused, "and all I can think is... I have not always been so good. I think... if I do not recover..." She paused, then asked, "Will I go to hell?"

Though chilled by her words, VonCosel reassured her as usual. "My dear, beautiful girl," he said, "I cannot even imagine such a thing."

Though the activity of drawing blood was routine, the moment was not. Finally, something had changed, and VonCosel claims to have felt it as intensely as he claims to have ever felt anything. It was almost all he could do to ready the needle. Yet rather than drawing blood, he drew some of the strange liquid from the vial Elena had noticed into his syringe.

Suddenly, Elena looked again at the strange liquid with a new and unexplained sense of understanding. After briefly looking around at her humble surroundings and even watching as Aurora passed by an open doorway across the room, she looked again at VonCosel and gently nodded.

With that, VonCosel says he slipped the needle into Elena's arm. With the syringe emptied, he slowly withdrew his injection hand while dabbing at the prick mark with his handkerchief. Never taking his eyes off of her, he sat back in his little wooden chair as the young woman quickly re positioned herself, weakly stretching out her limbs as best she could as if settling in for a long sleep.

She tried to manage one last look at her caretaker, but her eyes began to flutter. She tried to turn her face back up to the ceiling, but her chin kept falling down to her chest. "Do not fight it, my darling" VonCosel whispered, hopeful that he was heard only by Elena, herself.

Whether it was due to the unusual quiet that seemed to pervade the Hoyos household or simply intuition - or even a sixth sense - VonCosel turned to see Aurora walking into the room. On her heels was Florinda Hoyos Medina, Elena's older sister nicknamed Nana, still absently drying a plate in her hands as she peered around her mother with the same inquisitive and even slightly accusatory look that VonCosel had seen before.

Both women rushed to Elena's side and tried desperately to jostle her back to consciousness, repeating Elena's name over and over, but it was too late. Even the loud barking of the little family dog was obviously in vain.

"It was meant to be," VonCosel told me of the heart wrenching moment as he recalled it. "It was all meant to be."

At last, it seemed, she was gone. The flame was extinguished.

For VonCosel, the next few days were like sleep-walking through a nightmare. So distraught was the Hoyos family that they immediately charged VonCosel with care for Elena's body, which he promptly removed from the household. Having seen the vial and empty syringe next to Elena, they even forgot to ask what it was VonCosel had injected her with in Elena's final moments. It was medicine, they speculated – or so VonCosel believes. It didn't work, but ironically, the fact that the Hoyos family ceased expecting anything to work actually spared him a fair amount of suspicion.

However small Elena's world may have seemed to her in her final weeks and days, the world of Key West had more than a passing awareness of this local beauty. Recently, she had accompanied her father on a car ride about town during which Elena summoned what strength she had to wave to people out the passenger's window. This, like other activities, had been discouraged by VonCosel in Elena's condition, but the family still refused to fully listen let alone hear and heed his warnings. By then, he could not expect them to start, no matter how disturbing the inevitable consequences.

The proceedings, though inherently sad, were beautiful according to VonCosel, who was solely responsible for all arrangements and associated costs. At the time, nobody questioned him on any of it, and Elena's humble, lightweight casket was laid in its shallow, sandy grave in Key West's crowded cemetery.

VonCosel became openly nervous about the placement of Elena's grave. The thought of her exposure to the elements, he would tell the family, was almost too hard to bear; so in the days to come – and with the help of Nana's husband Mario - he would conceive and commission the construction of a small, but ornate mausoleum designed specifically to house Elena's body in what would also be an all new, much more ornate and elaborate coffin.

Then came the twist. VonCosel recalled the brisk walk home from the burial and the urgency with which he bounded up the steps of his new seaside home. Approaching his bedroom, he could see through its open door what he had waited to see all day.

Upon his modest bed lay a sleeping, yet breathing beauty he knew all too well. It was his unofficial child bride - Elena Hoyos!

CHAPTER THREE

VonCosel says that as Elena finally awoke, he was aroused as never before. At last, they could be together, free from the prying eyes of the Hoyos family and their bothersome and petty misfortune. He could never hate that which had brought Elena into the world, VonCosel says, but approve of her family he did not – nor did they of him.

"How do you feel, my darling?" VonCosel asked, standing at the foot of his bed as Elena slowly woke and began to sit up. He says that her first attempts to make eye contact were less than successful due to lingering effects of the injection, but she could hear him, and they both knew the score. "Somos libres, mi amor," he recalls saying. "We're free. We are finally free."

With that, Elena seemed to come out of her haze as if slipping out of a dress. She sat up straight in the bed, folded her knees to her chest as she wrapped her arms around them, then looked with uncharacteristic awareness and intensity into VonCosel's eyes as she said in his native tongue for once, "Danke, herr doktor. Danke."

*   *   *

As VonCosel describes it, their life was a dream, and one nobody suspected. Out of friendship, which had developed out of some necessity, he considered telling Elena's brother-in-law Mario, but the days immediately following her awakening was their honeymoon, he believed, and one not to be shared in any way, shape, or form.

Because they now lived so close to the ocean, he and Elena would begin and end most days with a walk on the shore. On occasion, she and VonCosel slowly waded into the ocean hand-in-hand. VonCosel noted with mild unease that Elena would always wear the same clothes and a flower in her hair often held by a headband. Then again, her family was poor, so except for whatever VonCosel gave her, she had little even in the way of clothing. It aroused his curiosity, but not enough to act upon. Once they were waist deep in salt water, he says, it was as if all but the waves and the sky had ceased their hustle and bustle simply to allow and to witness their kiss.

At first, their banter was playful and carefree. It was the life he had always wanted, and more, it was the life he had dreamed of providing for Elena. Eventually, though, the conversation would turn and... evolve. Eventually, they would have to discuss what had happened and what they, two, had done.

"So, what is it?" Elena asked. "What did you inject me with?"

"Tetrodotoxin from the puffer fish mixed with a sedative. It's usually found in the Pacific and is a strong paralytic. It is deadly beyond even the smallest of amounts, so one must be well-trained in its proper use. It sometimes simulates death and can last anywhere from a few hours to a few days. The sedative, of course, was to keep you from having to be conscious for it all."

"You must be skilled," Elena said, seeming to fully comprehend his words. "Except for my cold, I feel fine," she continued, "though I can't help but worry about mi familia - mama and papa, my sisters..."

Using the casual, American translation of her name, VonCosel explained. "Tuberculosis kills, Helen. It's a harsh reality, but one your family knew to prepare for."

VonCosel recalls beginning to feel worried, though at first, it was only that their newly found intimacy would morph into the cold familiarity of most married couples. He worried mostly that explanations like his would begin to offend Elena and finally cue her in as to how truly uncomfortable he was with her family and their ways. Even with said family out of the picture, they would never be out of Elena's heart, and the last thing VonCosel ever wanted was to hurt her.

Nothing was ever more real to me than Elena, but it was as if she existed to me as an entity unto herself. This fact went back to my childhood, to before Elena was born, so why should it ever change? Perhaps that was the root of my insensitivity when it came to her family. Beyond sympathy for what they were going through both financially and with a family member's illness, they were obstacles to me and to Elena, as I had blamed them for Elena's lack of recovery. In my eyes, whether true or not, they were the cause of every setback in our relationship.

Finally alone together, VonCosel began to wonder who Elena might be without her close-knit clan. This bothered him because up to then, he had always assumed that he knew her so well, as if she had been created exclusively for him and he should instinctively know everything about her. To what should have been his relief, though, there were few if any surprises as their time together passed. Still, it only gnawed at him more.

"They're hurting, Carl," Elena once said, referring to her family while sitting with VonCosel outside a Mallory Square cafe. News had come that illness was striking again.

History could be repeating itself, at least from the family's perspective.

"The whole world is hurting, my darling," VonCosel replied, careful to avoid remarking too pointedly or too honestly on the family Elena still loved.. and missed. "My home country has suffered for decades," he continued, "though I fear the worst is yet to come for the fatherland. Wilhelm may have been little more than a mockery of power and an easy target of blame for much of the Great War, yet my people are now desperate for more than a leader. They want a savior, someone to unify them and restore meaning to their lives in a world that would probably prefer they not exist. It appears that someone is stepping into that role and the people could be getting what they want, yet I still pity them. If you ask me, there is nothing more dangerous to a free people than an alleged savior."

Elena looked up at VonCosel and nodded. She knew that her own little country had struggled in the last few decades for more independence and recognition and so forth, but she hardly knew the details or even why. What she did know, apparently, was VonCosel. With but a look, she could reassure him of her love and the fact that she would... and could... never leave.

Then... "Was this what you wanted?" The all too familiar question was being asked in a woman's voice which made VonCosel tense-up and look around. Quickly, though, he found that the question came from their waitress, who continued by addressing him as, "Doctor?"

It was odd to hear from a stranger. Even in his job at the Marine Hospital, VonCosel was never actually a physician, though he did often go by the title and name of Doctor VonCosel. He glanced up at the waitress with an expression of frustration not dissimilar from the one he had when addressing the nurse on that fateful day when he and Elena had first met.

"Is there anything else I can get for either of you?" the waitress asked, trying to keep her cool despite VonCosel's withering gaze.

But VonCosel could not help himself. "What are you...?" he began asking when, suddenly, he was stopped by the touch of Elena's small hand on his. Immediately, he jerked his head back around and looked into Elena's eyes, which told him in no uncertain terms that everything was okay. He need not be unnerved. With that, the waitress seemed to disappear, and curiously enough, so did VonCosel's recollection of the rest of the outing... save for one thing.

After all this time, Elena was still wearing the exact same clothes, and the flower in her hair – natural as always – was still in bloom.

*   *   *

The house VonCosel remembers living in with Elena by the sea was a 2 story remnant from the previous century and a nod to more European tastes. The salty breeze that always seemed to be blowing lightly from the ocean had lent a cracked and weathered look to the home's wooden exterior and its pastel colors. Still, it sufficed, and it was home no matter what because Elena was there.

VonCosel recalls having serenaded Elena in their bedroom with one of several organs he had, which contained parts he had built or fixed, himself. Organs are yet another hobby for VonCosel from his youth, both in their playing and their construction. Naturally, he enjoyed the classics by the likes of Johann Sebastian Bach, Wolfgang Amadeus Mozart, Ludwig Von Beethoven, and of course, Richard Wagner.

Though not at all unusual for the Keys, VonCosel recalls one particular day when he noticed the skies outside begin to darken and a drizzle begin pelting the little window overlooking their bed. Either the organ music got old, or VonCosel got tired of playing, and so the two cuddled up together in the bed just barely large enough for both.

The room, though small, was sparse save for the bed and the organ. On its wall was one of VonCosel's diplomas as well as a picture of his recently deceased mother, a crucifix and, of course, a picture of Saint Cecelia. An old dresser contained what few casual clothes VonCosel owned while a small closet held one or two suits. Beside the bed was a bedside table, of course, but it remained empty. Besides a small lamp, only one rather peculiar item sat atop it: A small vial of the tetrodotoxin with which he had injected Elena to pull off their spectacular ruse.

That ruse, however, was beginning to make VonCosel feel more and more uncomfortable. Had it been too easy, he wondered? Was there something they had overlooked? Is Nana or Pancho Hoyos watching them from afar, waiting to strike? It felt like paranoia, but still justified.

Elena, of course, was still her same sweet self – right down to the clothes which she continued to wear even in bed! VonCosel could feel the warmth of her young body as she rested her head on his shoulder and draped her arm across his chest. Still, he was uneasy. Perhaps it was the rain, he recalls thinking. It was getting heavier and could easily turn into a storm.

"How is your cold,?" he asked. "Better?"

"I told you, I feel fine. Besides, I'm with you, aren't I? We fooled them, didn't we? Relax, my love. We're together now." Somehow, she knew what VonCosel needed to be reassured about beyond her alleged cold, and in a way, that disturbed him even more.

"Forgive me, Helen," he began, "but I must ask. Would you ever leave me?"

Elena raised her head slightly. "Why would you ask such a thing?"

"Please. The hard part is over. It's just that... well, you're so young still. I just have to hear it. Whatever you say, my darling, I'll believe you. Just tell me."

Elena withdrew the arm from over VonCosel's chest and used the other to prop herself up as she looked into VonCosel's eyes and spoke with a seriousness and even a hint of urgency which seemed almost wholly uncharacteristic of the Elena VonCosel knew. "I couldn't leave you, Carl," she said. "You know that."

"What do you mean?"

"Please, no more questions," Elena said with a sigh as she laid back down in her previous position.

Though he had hoped for an answer, VonCosel tried to let it go by putting one of his arms over Elena, but when he did, he inexplicably felt that something was wrong. "Elena," he began, "if you love me, you'll answer me true."

"But I did," Elena moaned. "You already know."

"You can't leave me," VonCosel said, withdrawing his arm. "You already said that, but..."

"You already know, beloved," Elena said as she sat up, her almost dark countenance contrasting with her affectionate words. "I can't leave."

"You can't? Why can't you?" VonCosel was frustrated – angry, even, and with Elena, which he had not even believed possible up to then. "Why do you keep saying that?" What does it even... mean?"

Then, an uneasy realization crept over VonCosel and was reflected in his facial expression, to which Elena could be seen reacting with her own, but hers was more one of knowing disappointment. She remained perfectly still, VonCosel recalls, though tears began streaming from her eyes.

"Why are you crying?" VonCosel asked, beginning to feel light-headed. "Elena? Why... why can't... can't you leave?"

VonCosel tried to blink away his disorientation, but the feeling only increased and was accompanied by sudden fatigue. "What...?" VonCosel tried to talk again, but he couldn't. Something was happening to him, and the usually fidgety Elena had not moved in what felt like more than 30 seconds. Her tearful gaze was still fixed upon him.

Then, she spoke. "Because, I..." The last movement VonCosel recalls seeing her make was when she hung her head, then looked back up at him, leaned into his face, and whispered the one explanation that had never occurred to him. "Because... I was never here."

CHAPTER FOUR

 T he most effective and insidious lie is not just the one with the most truth, but also the kind we most often tell ourselves. Look hard enough at the human condition and it becomes apparent just how much we depend on these lies in whatever form they may come.

It could be argued that upon those lies, we base and build everything from our interpersonal relationships to the societies in which we live. The only thing we truly need in this life is to survive, but our sentience demands more. Meaning, purpose, love... all mere constructs of our psyche which counter our self-destructive nature and motivate us to continue and prosper.

Ironically, the lie that VonCosel could not help telling himself and believing had come in the form of a dream. One moment, he was listening to Elena's voice while lounging with her in their bed in a nice, 2-story home by the sea. The next moment, he was waking up in a similar bed, but a totally different environment.

Instead of a two-story house, it was a small, wooden shack on Flagler Avenue which had outside of it a sign with the words *Dr. VonCosel's Laboratory*. Instead of *Carl VonCosel*, the name on the diploma hung precariously on his wall read *Karl Tanzler* - the supposed doctor to which he recalled the Marine Hospital nurse referring as she handed him Elena's test results. That is, it was the one referred to in his dream. Like the man in Kafka's *Metamorphosis*, Karl was in shock at his own – or, rather, at the man he really was. He told me that the shock was as physical as it was emotional.

As clearly as I see and hear you now, I had watched as Elena leaned over me, and with tears in her eyes, answered my question. Because, she said, I was never here. Again, my eyes fluttered, and when they reopened, I was alone - totally and utterly alone. All of our time together, away from her family - our plans, our walks, our talks, our private world - it had all been a dream. A fantasy. A delusion.

Beside him was a bedside table, but it was old and rickety, and there was no vial of tetrodotoxin. Instead, there sat a stained handkerchief which he recognized all too well and was a chilling symbol of his most horrifying revelation.

Elena was dead and he was totally alone.

The loneliness and guilt came upon me like a wave which began sucking the breath from my body. I gasped for air as I watched the facts replayed in my head.

Karl had never injected Elena with the death-mimicking toxin. It had merely been another drawing of Elena's blood for analysis, and they spoke very little if at all because Elena could hardly breathe or control her own coughing.

In his new recollection, the blood was drawn and Karl was standing, backing away as Elena began coughing uncontrollably. The little dog began barking as Aurora and Florinda entered the room. Aurora knelt at her daughter's side, but she was helpless to do more than wipe blood from around her daughter's mouth.

Suddenly, Karl recalled standing in the Hoyos doorway, looking through and past a crowd of relatives and friends to Elena, who sat in a wooden chair in one corner of the room, startlingly pale and motionless... gazing past him.

Gazing into infinity. Her sisters were trying to revive her, but it was clearly too late. It apparently had been for some time and most seemed to instinctively know that even if they didn't want to admit it.

After a second, Pancho Hoyos was recalled begging Karl to take control and pay for arrangements which the Hoyos family could not afford. In his mind, Karl could see the grief-stricken father's mouth moving, but heard no words. Instead, his mind set everything to the classical music that Karl had grown up with – Berlioz or, more fittingly, a requiem mass. Mozart's, probably. He could not recall.

Finally, he found himself outside, in a procession following Elena's small, wooden coffin through the Key West cemetery to its inevitably shallow resting place. In his mind, Karl watched again in horror as it was lowered into the grave and just barely covered with dirt and sand. Karl knew it was never going to be enough to protect the coffin or Elena's body from the elements, and that fact was almost more than he could bear.

Eventually, the memories and their intensity subsided. Karl could breathe again, but it was no real relief. Elena was still gone. 'Not coming back. And almost as bad was the realization that everything – the deception of the faked death, the glorious seaside honeymoon, the intimate moments in bed together – had not only been an intensely real dream, but a recurring one which not only convinced Karl of events that did not happen, but of an identity he did not really possess.

No longer was I the noble Count descended from the Countess VonCosel and destined for a great love affair. As my diploma now clearly read, I was George Karl Tanzler, the bacteriologist that was banished from his homeland by foolish war, had abandoned his real family for adventure, and who had loved a woman that could not love me back and who had indeed died in my care. In the moment, I reasoned only that if the pain from this rude awakening did not finally kill me, I would surely finish the job, myself.

Karl had experienced this dream before, but it had never been this intense. As he sat on his wooden floor next to the bed, barely able to find the will or the strength to pick himself up, he contemplated his own death. As he put it:

I was never one to discount the dream life as merely a temporary delusion or altered mental state. Life, itself, hinges on our ability to perceive the world around us, but who is to say that we ever perceive it correctly? Like one who sees shapes in the clouds or an intruder when there is none, who is to say that our perception is any more accurate when we are awake than when are dreaming? We do not necessarily see things as they are, but as light presents them to us, creating both the color and the shadow and even motion and the illusion thereof. What, then, is the shape and texture of the world devoid of light? To us, it is darkness – that which we first see when we close our eyes. What is the world's sound? Without our ears or vibrations to ripple through them, it is nothing. All is darkness. All is silence.

Nevertheless, this could not comfort me. The intricacies of perception could not change the fact that I was alone. Elena was not with me, either physically or in any other perceptible form. That being so, it occurred to me to ask what I was without her.

My life had been an adventure up to then, but it was an adventure I had taken almost entirely alone – yet secure in the knowledge that Elena and I would one day meet and I would be alone no more. Even my marriage to Doris was a ruse – a compromise to satiate and distract me until I encountered the one with whom I was truly meant to share my life. For better or worse, that is partly why I left Doris and our two little girls.

As much as it pained me to know how I hurt them, I realized that I was of no more use to them in their presence than out of it – not so long as I knew my life was incomplete. Whatever drew me further South to the Keys must have known that it was time – that within three years and after more than half of my life had no doubt passed, I would finally encounter my soul mate. Still, I wondered. Did it also know how fate would as swiftly yank said soul mate away from me?

Like our initial meeting, perhaps it was providence that with the ending of her life, mine was meant to end soon thereafter. There is, after all, something else which awaits us – another plane of existence not anchored to the physical. Though I did not know how it would be accomplished, I felt strongly that I would once again be in Elena's presence very soon. There, on the floor, I sat waiting to be told by fate, the spirits, or even Elena, herself, how I could affect the end of my own life in this world so that I could start one with Elena in the next.

It was then, Karl said, that he got his answer, which allegedly came from Elena, herself!

Just as I thought I could will my own demise, my breathing steadied, my mind and ears opened up, and I heard her voice - soft, almost childlike as ever, and calling my name. In my ignorance, I had entombed her seemingly lifeless body with an essence that could not be extinguished. Like the bittersweet refrain of a symphonic requiem, I heard the only two words needed to spur me to action. Rescue me, she said.

Rescue me.

*   *   *

It was at this point that Karl stopped, pointing out that most of what happened next had become public knowledge and that I was not likely to believe his version of events, anyway. This was on my second visit and I could have easily left as the guard and now the Sheriff wanted. As sympathetic as he was, the increasing amount of attention from the press and other visitors was becoming more than even the Sheriff was willing to deal with on Karl's behalf. They did not need me adding to the stress.

As you know, however, I am not one to back down easily. I made my case both to Karl and to the Sheriff, whose orders the contentious and heavily accented guard had to take. My case was simply that Karl's story up to Elena's death was mere pretense. I was interested in everything that came thereafter – everything they thought they knew about what Karl had done and why he was sitting in jail in the first place. Surely, I thought to myself, there was more to this than I had been told.

"I do not wish to be rude," Karl began, "But as you can surely see, the world is not ready to understand – to truly understand – what happened next."

Naturally, I protested. "And with all due respect, Karl, that makes no sense to me. Besides, if I'm to go home with a valid story, I'll need more than just this stuff about an otherwise run-of-the-mill affair that may or may not have even taken place the way in which you described." In my mind, I knew that it had not been run-of-the-mill. Given the age and even racial and cultural difference, the mere suggestion of one must have bordered on the scandalous.

Nevertheless, I again felt I needed to engage in a bit of emotional trickery in order to guide Karl to a place in his own psyche where he would not only want, but need to continue his story. After all, I thought, nobody that had ever had as grandiose a self-image as did Karl Tanzler could ever pass up the chance for more and more attention. And it worked.

"If I tell you what happened next," he said, "do I have your word that you will report on it honestly?"

"I have not been able to record your voice," I began, "so I cannot quote you word-for-word. But, other than that... yes, I promise."

It was at that moment when that irksome young guard showed up, supposedly checking on us – no doubt checking to see if he could find reason to run me out. I turned my head and glared at him, as did Karl as best he could through the bars. I'm not sure why, but the guard merely shook his head and left.

"That guard... He doesn't like us,"

"He doesn't like me," Karl said. "He thinks me a, uh... how did he put it? A dirty old man... If I recall, those were his exact words when I was first brought in."

"All the more reason to continue your story, then, no?" At that, Karl glared at me through the bars and I suspected that he suspected that I had manipulated him into continuing. For a moment, I feared this to not only be true, but to be the one thing that could change his mind. But, I needn't have worried. Karl is nothing if not compulsive.

"Whether you believe me about hearing Elena calling out to me or not," he began, "surely you can understand my concern about her body having been placed in that terribly shallow grave. Granted, it's really the only kind of grave we have here in Key West due to the fact that we are literally at or below sea level. Still, most are covered in concrete with some heavy, concrete statue or other such sculpture atop it, usually at its head. This was not so with Elena.

"Luckily," he continued, "I had been put in charge of pretty much all of her arrangements. Initially, I had been too overwhelmed with grief to think of it, but now, I thought about and was willing and able to remedy the situation."

That remedy came in the form of a relatively small, but semi-ornate mausoleum designed specifically to hold Elena's body and, at some point in the future, Karl's body, too. There has been much talk, apparently, about the mausoleum's peculiar features, including a phone line allegedly run to and even in Elena's coffin, which was also new and supposedly custom-built to Karl's specifications. People believe that this was meant to allow Karl to talk to Elena, directly, without having to actually be inside.

It's an undisputed fact that Karl visited the ornate tomb every evening, bringing with him one or more flowers and sitting just outside the door to the mausoleum for what seemed an extended period of time to those that claim to have seen him. It was during this time that his elaborate recurring dream supposedly... recurred... and at the end of it, Karl says, he not only heard Elena speak to him.

He heard her sing.

*   *   *

There was a lover that, due to bad luck, had his sweet beloved taken by the Reaper. Every night he went to the cemetery to visit his beauty's grave.

The song is called La Boda Negra, and to Karl, the lyrics he heard Elena sing were clear instructions of what to do next. By then, approximately two years had passed since

Elena's death, but the compulsion was too great to resist. Ever the open-minded scientist, Karl was determined that he and Elena would have the marriage and the life for which he still believed they were destined... even if he had to break the laws of God and man to achieve it!

It was late one evening in April of 1933 that Karl, armed with the keys and a child's red wagon, marched through Key West's lush and crowded cemetery to Elena's mausoleum. Having opened the door, he ducked inside and began the unenviable task of removing Elena's coffin, which he just barely managed to hoist onto the wagon and tug back the way he came. He claims to have seen spirits all around, including Elena's as she supposedly guided him in the darkness until he reached the gate. He likened the mood to a celebration – a wedding celebration, no less – with the apparitions of deceased Key West citizens cheering and urging him on.

At this point in his tale, I began to wonder what I had gotten myself into and whose trust I had really worked to earn. This is the sort of information that has not been made public, as yet, and it seemed to be for good reason. While I should have expected this and knew what came next, I still found myself ill-prepared for the details.

At some point – and Karl is a bit vague on this – the coffin fell off the wagon and deposited Elena's tightly wrapped, yet still moist and rapidly decomposing body onto the ground. Because of the island's incessantly high temperatures, it was a miracle if Elena was in as good a condition as Karl eventually described. That would only have been possible because of the lengths to which Karl had gone when he had her moved to the new, more ornate coffin, which had supposedly been filled with formaldehyde before being placed into the mausoleum. While he insists that this was not the case, it is almost as if he knew exactly what he would later do when he hired Elena's brother-in-law Mario and some others to build what was supposed to have been Elena's final resting place.

As of that night in 1933, however, Karl was determined that his darling girl would be near to him at all times. So determined was he that when the coffin spilled Elena's body onto the ground, he supposedly slung her corpse over his shoulder and climbed the fence. He even claims to have hailed a cab at that late hour without ever drawing significant suspicion as to the nature of his rather large and suspicious luggage.

What he did with the coffin is still a mystery to me, as is the reason nobody seems to have noticed what he had done, but however it happened, Karl managed to cart Elena's body over the island and to his would-be airplane first, where he stored it for a day or two before finally moving it to the shack on Flagler.

He wasted no time getting to work on the difficult task ahead, which he said was not merely to restore Elena's physical body as best he could. Thanks to the confidence he had in his own knowledge of electronic and radioactive gadgetry as well as his self-proclaimed medical prowess, he also felt that he could reasonably restore to Elena that which had seemingly been taken far too soon.

Her Earthly life!

*   *   *

Having relayed Karl's outlandish goal of bringing Elena back to life, I want to be clear about just what kind of "life" Karl imagined he could restore... or, rather, substitute for the one Elena originally had. This is where those narrow definitions become relevant – the ones he attributes to just about everybody else in the world. Many have said that the dead speak to us, metaphorically, but Karl believes that they could do so in a more literal sense... just much, much, much slower. He believes that we deny the dead enough time to... recover, if you will... and that the real death comes needlessly after we have taken and silenced them either by burial or cremation.

Karl obviously believes that resurrection was possible with Elena. That belief is easily ridiculed, yet Karl believed it so strongly that he acted on it in ways most would have a hard time imagining. This is why I say that cold, hard fact is almost incidental. The latest bizarre, yet undisputed facts of this case are only possible because of what many would say is Karl's hyperactive imagination combined with his chillingly pervasive obsession with romancing she who was still, even in death, Mrs. Maria Elena Millagro Hoyos Mesa.

The process of retrieval and restoration, as he calls it, was a difficult one. He described to me his mindset and perspective at the time.

In hindsight, I should have feared getting caught that evening in April, yet I was propelled by an almost frightening certainty that what I was doing was right. The cemetery had been filled with the spirits of the dead rejoicing at our reunion and my head was still filled with the sound of Elena singing to me of her desire to be rescued and guiding me as I brought her home. Having stored her there for a day or two out of necessity, I could not wait to retrieve her from my makeshift plane. In the meantime, I prepared my home on Flagler as best I could, filling it with the tools and instruments I would need and even building a special bed for Elena and the job at hand.

That job was tedious and taxing, to say the least. It began with the disheartening process of seeing just for myself what ravages the grave had wrought upon the body of my beautiful girl. I had taken steps to preserve it as best I could, but the heat, humidity, and other natural conditions had still been unrelenting. Maggots latched themselves to the linen in which she was wrapped and to the visible bits of skin which was now clearly discolored and rotting. Much of her skin had to be replaced with a combination of silk and plaster . Her hair was falling out in clumps and her body seemed to be sinking in upon itself. This I used for her wig, which also consisted of bits of hair given to me upon Elena's death by her mother as a sort of partial memento mori, if you will. As you know, these have traditionally been photographs which, for some reason, have only begun to disappear as one of our shared traditions since the advent of the current century, less romantic century.

There were times I felt like giving up – times I wondered what I was doing and why – but then, there she was, always in my head, reminding me of all we had been through and of the future we deserved... the future we would share together.

CHAPTER FIVE

After days of strenuous and frankly disturbing work, Karl was exhausted and his nerves were frayed. He had created a wig from clumps of Elena's hair, which fell from her dried-up scalp, and used piano wire to repair and reconnect limbs. Every time he would leave and come back with boxes of perfume to mask the pervasive odor, he feared being spotted by an overly suspicious neighbor. Every time he went into town, he feared encountering and having to explain what he was doing to a member of the Hoyos family, particularly if that family member was Elena's big sister Nana. Her husband Mario, however, would prove to be a different story. In time, Karl would have to confide in him in order to ask for help, usually when it came to home repairs. Fortunately, Mario tended to mind his own business and, in this case, knew the necessity of keeping the truth from his already suspicious wife.

When the job was finally done, Karl found a moment alone with his reconstructed companion. He collapsed out of fatigue as he was physically and emotionally spent, but that was not the worst of it. Silence had befallen him, and doubt had crept back in.

A couple of days earlier, Karl suddenly found that he could no longer Elena in his mind. Under the circumstances, it was startling and disturbing. Now, the silence was actually beginning to take a toll. For the first time, he began questioning everything he had done.

Could he have been wrong? It seemed unthinkable. After all, how could God allow him to encounter and fall in love with the literal girl of his dreams only to have him spend almost all of their time together watching her deteriorate and die? What had he done to this poor family? Had he really seduced them with empty promises just so he could lend meaning to hallucinations and feed his own lust?

Perhaps these doubts were the wages of sin - emotional penance for abandoning his real family to pursue a relationship that would meet only his needs and satisfy only his requirements for a life-long companion. In that moment, he looked upon his work and for a second, he felt embarrassed, ashamed, and even nauseous at the true horror of it all.

In the mirror, he saw what the pursuit had done to him. His hair was thin and white, his beard overgrown, and both his face and body were now gaunt from being malnourished. This was not the man that Karl's very proper German family had raised him to be. This was not the boy on whom his mother had doted while his sisters playfully giggled at his backyard experiments with kites and all manner of homemade devices.

Either from exhaustion or guilt, or both, Karl collapsed upon the bed next to Elena's lifeless and heavily modified form. He began sobbing uncontrollably and once gasped in fright when he accidentally touched his cold, stiff bride. He worried that his sobs might be heard, particularly by the ocean-obsessed transient that had become his on-again, off-again roommate, but even that could not bring him back to composure.

Karl longed to hear Elena's voice again. Her youth and vitality, however fleeting the latter may have been, was like an intoxicant to Karl and a distraction from the growing realization that he had lived more than half of his life already – and in that time, what had he accomplished? For what would he be remembered were he remembered at all? Would he receive credit for his intellect and ingenuity? Or would he ultimately be known as the lovesick freak that burned through two thirds of his time on Earth in pursuit of a romantic illusion, then spent the last in a fool's quest to make it as real as possible?

Finally, the comforting notion dawned on him that none of that mattered. Our bodies invariably turn to dust, so what value could the universe see in what we do with them? If he had lived his life only to be with another, why was that such a bad thing?

At long last, he and Elena were together. If the circumstances were not ideal, it was but a trivial glitch that would remedy itself when Karl's time came and he would rejoin Elena in the grave. And it would not be just any grave, but the same little mausoleum that he had built and from which he had recently fetched her body.

For the next few years, Karl could be said to have been living in solitude, yet to Karl, nothing could have been further from the truth. Besides the transient and the intermittent contact with Elena's brother-in-law Mario, he had Elena, herself – though he knew that none would believe an honest account of their time together. In that time, he was forced to play a veritable game to preserve Elena's body and keep their relationship a secret. He was forced to make due with little in his daily life while avoiding or weathering everything from the queries and suspicions of neighbors to the particularly bad hurricane of 1935.

Still, it was worth it. The doubt and shame he had felt immediately upon completing Elena's physical restoration was now only a memory, one chalked up to fatigue and a therefore stressed and unreasoning mind. He was forced to quit his job at the Marine Hospital, but otherwise, his life was not so unusual... or so he believed. Like others, he worked and ran errands in the day, slept at night, and even fished a little out of the warm Atlantic Ocean.

Life was good for George Karl Tanzler, who occasionally still thought of himself as and even went by the name Count VonCosel. As long as he had Elena, he reasoned, it would stay good. And, after five or six years, it was becoming far less likely that anyone would stumble upon his... *their*... little secret.

That is, of course, until it actually happened.

*   *   *

Reports are conflicted on just how Florinda "Nana" Hoyos Medina found out, but perhaps it was inevitable that she be the one to do so. Karl believes that her appearance at his house followed an alleged attempt to steal the jewelry with which Elena had been entombed. At that point, Nana would have seen that the mausoleum was empty and done exactly what she did, which was to show up at Karl's home demanding to know where Elena's body was.

As I write this, the details are to be sorted out at the upcoming hearing, but it was earlier this month, in October of 1940, when Nana showed up on Karl's doorstep and more or less forced her way inside to ascertain Elena's whereabouts. Upon seeing her sister's modified corpse, she is alleged to have believed it some kind of doll. With a straight face and as much compassion and reassurance as he could muster, Karl says he finally convinced poor Nana of the truth. After almost nine full years, this was, indeed, her little sister, her countenance poorly simulated with plaster, silk, and glass eyes that forever stare upwards into eternity.

Despite having expected something foul and alerted police, Florinda shrieked in horror and anguish when faced with the grim reality of it all. Even Karl knew that Nana must have wondered how anyone could do such a thing, yet he seems to have underestimated how strongly she would react.

To him, it was perfectly fine. It was not as if he, himself, had killed her, and because they were so poor at the time, the Hoyos family had given him total control over Elena's final arrangements, which included her body and what would be done with it. Besides, Karl loved Elena. He had made no effort to hide that fact. While this was not something to be shared freely or in mixed company, neither was it harming Elena's family or anyone else. As for Elena, herself, surely Karl's actions could not be construed as any worse or more disrespectful than the act of embalming. That process goes all the way back to the ancient Egyptians and was locally revised and modernized in the mid-nineteenth century.

And yet, Karl soon found himself handcuffed and standing in his own front yard, staring at his humble shack on Flagler Avenue as police officers and the coroner removed Elena in what appeared to be some kind of wicker basket. It was all Karl could do to watch as the woman he loved was literally stolen from him by local law enforcement. The Sheriff acted as if he was sympathetic, and Karl believes that he was, but it is more likely that Karl was being placated and patronized.

There, in the hot Key West sun, Karl stood and watched as his life of seven years was dismantled and effectively ended within the span of a few minutes. His eyes were beginning to swell with tears when, to his bittersweet relief, he saw Elena for the very last time. As he believes she had appeared to him long before they actually met, her spirit appeared to him that day as beautiful as ever, walking on her own two legs just ahead of the basket that carried her Earthly corpse.

For Karl, it was as if time slowed down just long enough for Elena to look him in the eyes as she approached. Then, without stopping, she slowed down, turned her head and whispered something into one of Karl's ears. After that, he says, he did not even try to turn his head to see if she would still be visible. What Elena or her spirit whispered to him as that basket was carried by was exactly what Karl needed to hear... what he had always needed to hear from her whenever he felt that something was wrong. "My darling," Elena said...

"Suffer this for me... one last time."

CHAPTER SIX

I said that I had changed by the time Karl's story ended, and I had. Until then, I was not entirely sure what it was about his story that drew me to it, nor was I likely to have acknowledged it had I known. As he came to the part about his arrest, however, I knew I was approaching my final few minutes with the man as that annoying guard was already eyeing me from the corner.

In my final few minutes, I wanted to get Karl's permission to tell his story in the form of a more personal editorial. Technically, I didn't need it, but I had discovered some things shortly before my final visit that made me feel obligated to ask permission first. Part of it was the answer to a question that I had earlier refused to hear, persuading me then and for all time that there really is a monster lurking in this tale... but it is not Karl Tanzler.

Disrespectful sensationalism is an unfortunate part of today's journalism. I made my peace with that years ago. What I found myself unable to be at peace with was what the relatively small community of Key West did upon discovering Karl's already disconcerting secret. The city did not merely remove Elena's body from Karl's house and perform an autopsy. Upon arriving at the Lopez Funeral home, workers restored Karl's work as best they could and displayed the poor girl's body for no fewer than 6,800 citizens – including schoolchildren that were actually let out of class early for this very reason!

No wonder the funeral home owner seemed surprised that I had not yet heard. The disturbing irony did not escape me. At the time, Karl Tanzler was sitting in jail, awaiting prosecution for the otherwise private and secretive desecration of a tomb he had built and a body for which the Hoyos family had freely given him responsibility. Meanwhile, the town that has the gall to all but destroy this poor man's life for doing something seven years prior, and which actually hurt nobody, was taking what he did a step further and most likely profiting from it.

It is one thing for newspapers like the Key West Citizen and Miami Herald to report the facts. It is another thing entirely to extend and expound upon the potential shame and embarrassment of both Karl Tanzler and the Hoyos family by publicly displaying their loved one's poorly restored corpse nine full years after her tragic and premature death!

"You can trust me," I told Karl in the moment or two before I had to leave for the last time. "I can tell your story – make people understand your side of things."

"It doesn't matter," he said. "All that matters is when I'll be reunited with Elena."

It took me a moment to think of what to say, but as before, I realized that honesty was my best choice. "Look, I understand where you're coming from. I felt the same way in '37. It was like... one day, we were together and happy. The next... he was gone. 'A casualty of a freak accident while working on the railroad. After a while, I learned to deal with it, but I don't think those feelings ever totally went away. I'm not sure they ever will.

"The thing is, we don't have to face these things alone. You pretty much hid yourself away with Elena for seven years because you feared people's reaction to what you had done. But believe it or not, the world outside isn't always so cruel. Now that the story is out, anyway, give the world a chance. Give me a chance to bring everyone around. Yours is like that Greek tragedy about the guy who retrieved his wife from the underworld only to see her yanked back down again when he looked back to see if she was really following him to the surface. I guarantee that people will understand – maybe not all, but many."

From Karl's facial expression, I believed I was getting through. "You're not alone, you know, and you don't have to be. Let me help you. Let me show people the truth... from the only perspective that really counts. Yours."

"Alone?" Karl began. "But dear Frau, I know I'm not alone. I realize that my Elena will always be with me, regardless of form. You wanted to know the truth? The truth is simple. We were in love, and when I finally looked behind to make sure she was there, they took her from me." He paused and looked directly into my eyes. "But not for long."

For a moment, I was dumbfounded. I knew he had made an impression on me, but I did not yet understand it well enough to truly perceive Karl's circumstances and tale as much more than the twisted combination of love, lust, and self-delusion. However, before I could talk again, that same guard came to usher me out of the jail. That was the last time I saw the man most knew as Count Carl VonCosel.

Since then, it has been a couple of weeks and I've not returned home. Neither have I contacted my editor. For some reason, I've felt compelled to stay in Key West and see what happens. I realize this could cost me my job and maybe more, but I simply cannot leave. As I'm sure you've surmised, this is far more than an assignment to me now. I must understand it – all of it. Doing so means being here to learn Karl's fate. At that time, I will pick up where I've left off.

*   *   *

It is December, 1940, and Karl Tanzler is free. The statute of limitations on grave robbery, which was the only viable charge, has run out. However, upon the dismissal of Karl's case, he was given mere hours to leave town... for good.

The last time I saw Karl, he was still in his jail cell. His final words caught me off guard. I was still convinced that I felt or should feel some sense of repulsion – if not towards the man, then towards his state of mind and what he had done.

Since then, I have experienced an almost total change of perspective – and apparently, so have many in America who have read or are reading about the case in their newspapers. My own morbid fascination with this story has transformed into a weird blend of pity and admiration for one that would go so far to not only be with the one he loves, but even attempt the impossible to restore that person to life. Now, I can be honest with myself and others.

Like Karl with Elena, I would do anything I could to have you back!

If Karl is right about anything, I believe it is that we do not understand human death half as well as we think we do. We disguise it, avoid it, cover it up, and shroud it in ritual, theology, and the very sort of delusions that are hypocritically chastised in everyday life. As a society, we cling to and obsess over these things even as similar obsessions in individuals are discouraged and stigmatized.

Ever since the time of the ancient Egyptians, societies like ours have found ever more creative ways of making the dead seem as if they are merely sleeping. Since the Civil War, modern embalming methods have become such that a corpse can look *acceptable* for weeks on-end. It takes its fair share of maintenance, but it can be and is done.

Still, for all that work, we eventually take the body and entomb it... bury it... and usually in some ornate casing that neither benefits the dead nor is seen by most in good condition for more than a few days or weeks. Sanitation is one thing, but our ways of dealing with the dead have become a cornucopia of waste. Yet, we justify it with the notion that the dead somehow deserve special respect and attention... at least, as long as it is convenient for us to give it.

All the while, we speak as if the dead are still alive in another realm. The ancient Egyptians believed that pharaohs and other worthy ones would go on to lead entire lives within the deep labyrinths and catacombs of their pyramids and tombs. Everyday trinkets would be combined with gold and other treasure, jewelry, scrolls, and walls covered in imagery and hieroglyphics meant to both guide and aid the dead in their new lives. In the far East, concubines would be murdered or even buried alive with recently deceased emperors.

In short, Karl Tanzler's reaction to Elena Hoyos' death and ensuing actions should barely phase us when considered in the context of more acceptable practices. His ideas of the physically dead still being able to communicate are barely more bizarre than many of our long-held beliefs about the afterlife. Though I am glad he is free and pleased by the apparent acceptance and understanding currently shown by much of the general public, I cannot seem to forgive the exploitation and double-standards with which both he and the Hoyos family have been treated by Key West and its officials. From top to bottom, this has been a private affair. It was for the better part of a decade, and but for the law and one woman's alleged greed, should have remained so.

I admit to being confused right now about my own life and what I will do. I intentionally failed to write and submit a story to my editor and have been unable to return to work, let alone my former, day-to-day life. No doubt I am fired by now, but I cannot bring myself to care.

My experiences in Key West have only made me miss you more. If only I could do what Karl did. I understand now how it could be enough to have someone back, if only in a certain form. And whether or not it is healthy or right, I know the single-mindedness of grief, regret, and anger towards the causes of all of it.

So impassioned was I that upon hearing of Karl's banishment from town, I waited until he had left and, then, used discreetly obtained explosives to destroy what had been Elena's mausoleum. Nobody knows I did it. They likely chalk it up to vandalism, or perhaps they blame Karl, himself. It would have been fitting had he set the structure to explode after his departure. For me, the act was a message. It was meant to tell Key West and its people that there would be nothing of original significance left with which they could further exploit or deride this man and the family he tried to serve.

Faith is a beautifully dangerous thing without which I fear our lives would have little meaning. Karl had faith that he could somehow achieve the life he always wanted with Elena even though she had physically died. Part of me still wonders how he could have taken that faith as far as he did, but I cannot hold it against him.

I hope you understand now why I relate this tale to you. I can only have faith that you have heard my words as I have written them. My path will be different, but I hold out hope that like that of Karl and Elena's, our connection remains. With no regret or remorse, I freely admit that it is my eternal obsession.

EPILOGUE

The preceding has been compiled and published as found in the form of a bound manuscript buried beneath the concrete floor of a shed behind a home in Columbia, South Carolina. Though records from the time cannot confirm, authorities believe that it was once the home of the manuscript's author: Agatha Patricia Leery.

Published as simply A.P., Leery had been a reporter and sometimes columnist for the publication Modern View. Friends and neighbors described her as what we would now call a "workaholic," so when she started dating and became engaged to Raymond Holmes in 1936, it was a pleasant surprise for everyone that knew her.

Sadly, Holmes was killed by an oncoming train while working on the railroads in 1937. Afterwards, Leery's editor recalls that she became moody, more combative, and frequently dissatisfied with her assignments for reasons that she could never sufficiently articulate. According to her editor, the assignment in Key West was not real. It was a minor story, anyway, and already being adequately covered. Though he later admitted regretting the action, which was questioned and criticized by peers at the time – including the Modern View's publisher - he thought it would be a good change of pace for Leery, distracting her from her own problems while also lending what he hoped to be some perspective. Instead, it seems to have only intensified an already troubled mindset, likely brought upon by a combination of grief and some untreated mental illness.

According to all recorded sources, the magazine received one wire from Leery announcing her first visit to Mr. Tanzler in jail. Despite having obviously returned at one point to bury her manuscript, she was never heard from by anyone that knew or worked with her again.

As for the home behind which the manuscript was found, evidence of it having been Leery's is limited to second-hand information about a friend of the family that had been letting Leery live there after moving away for work. The home was never in Leery's name, however, and no evidence exists to suggest that she returned to live there for any length of time.

Leery had been missing for over five years when the magazine folded in 1946. The case was briefly investigated in February of 1941, but by then, leads were unreliable and quickly grew cold. A guard at the jail in Key West recalled Leery's visits, but had nothing of substance to volunteer as to what might have happened to her. No evidence of foul play was ever found and her written confession of having supposedly blown up the mausoleum remains unsubstantiated.

The closest anyone has come to finding evidence explaining Leery's disappearance was in 1942 when a curious detective looked into the reports on Mr. Holmes' death. With railway safety a growing concern, the help of the Interstate Commerce Commission, or ICC, was sought by the train's manufacturer to help prove that the death was a suicide rather than an accident. Though the ICC declined, a private investigator supposedly discovered that Holmes had more than one mistress and may have even still been married – all while seeing Ms. Leery. One of the mistresses was supposedly a wealthy heiress who, upon discovering Holmes' other affairs, threw him out and threatened to expose his philandering.

No proof exists that Leery ever found out or was even contacted by participants in the investigation. However, the manufacturer unsuccessfully attempted to use the private findings to convince the coroner to change Holmes' cause of death from having been an accident to a suicide.

The company from which Holmes had bought life insurance sided with the coroner. The policy's beneficiary was Holmes' sister, though there was little to be inherited and the sister claimed to have been ignorant of the policy's existence. Though Leery, her actions, and her subsequent disappearance have never been tied directly to Holmes' death or the cause thereof, speculation exists that she eventually committed suicide out of lingering grief and anguish.

The latest and final lead to be explored in the case came shortly after this manuscript's discovery when, on a hunch, the Columbia, South Carolina, Sheriff's Department found and released documentation from 1941 of a complaint that Mr. Holmes' grave had been vandalized. Though an exhumation was requested once and denied by the court, the complaint was otherwise never followed-up.

Karl Tanzler, AKA Count Carl VonCosel, relocated to Florida to eventually reopen his own lab and live near his former wife. In addition to writing his own lengthy account of the Hoyos affair for a pulp magazine, he showed off his inventions to tourists and other visitors while telling them of his famous adventures and infamous affair. He died of natural causes in 1952 and was discovered in his home by police three weeks later alongside organ parts, sardine cans, and a life-sized effigy of what was and would forever be his child bride... Elena Hoyos.

- Publisher, 2016

ABOUT THE AUTHOR

Despite physical hardships since birth, JD Moores has a degree in communications and experience in film and video production in addition to his screenwriting activities. Other written works, most of which are commentaries on entertainment and popular culture, have been featured in books, magazines, and on web-sites and blogs.

Moores currently resides in North Florida. Find more at *http://www.jdmoores.com*.

www.ingramcontent.com/pod-product-compliance
Lightning Source LLC
Chambersburg PA
CBHW070647130626
46555CB00006B/2752